RACED BY HER LESBIAN BOSS

K.F. JONES

"Yes. Yes, that fits perfectly," Susanna said as she circled Amber, tugging a hem here, adjusting a lapel there.

"Does it? I've never worn this sort of outfit before."

"Not even when you went riding?"

"That was only a couple of times, and it was more of a tracksuit and trainers type of thing. It didn't compare to this," Amber replied, gesturing with her hands down the length of her body at the costume she was wearing. A costume or a uniform? She wasn't quite sure.

"How do the jodhpurs feel?"

"They're a bit tight. Are they too small?"

"Mmmm," Susanna murmured, running her hand down Amber's back and over the taut material stretched over her buttocks. Amber shivered and bit her lip. "No, I think they're fine. Try moving in them."

"Moving?"

"Yes, walk around a bit, see if you can bend over and touch your toes, that sort of thing," Susanna purred.

"Yes, Mistress," Amber answered. She did her best impression of a catwalk model, striding across the massive bedroom and turning on the ball of her foot before walking back. The thigh-length riding boots were fairly easy to walk in, despite the heels. She wasn't sure if they were quite right for riding, but they looked fantastic and accentuated her calves beautifully.

When she reached her mistress, she pulled up short and turned once more. Amber bent at the waist, reaching down and grasping her ankles. "How's that?"

"Provocative," Susanna said. "A perfect fit, in my not so humble opinion. The jacket too. Here's your helmet, and your carriage whip, use it sparingly and don't let me catch you with your helmet off while we're racing. Safety first."

"Of course, Mistress."

"Come on, it's time for breakfast and don't you dare get any marmalade on that jacket."

"Yes, Mistress."

❦

"Are we going to race now, Mistress?" Amber asked as she carefully folded the napkin she'd used to dab her lips clean of marmalade and toast crumbs. It had been an unusually light breakfast for her so perhaps Susanna had asked Pudding to keep it small as they would be exercising.

Susanna, however, shook her head, "No, you're going to come to the office with me. It's time you started working for your keep." Mistress stood up and smiled before heading to the door, "After all, you are my personal assistant, and that is a real job, not just fun and games, you know."

"Of course, Mistress," Amber replied as she followed behind.

"Good. You are here to carry out tasks so that I don't have to. You're not just here to be a source of amusement, no matter how sweetly you squeal when I punish you or how appealing I find your tears."

Amber took a gamble that this was rhetorical and remained silent as they made their way across the mansion to Susanna's office suite.

Susanna stopped in the spacious room outside her office and pointed to a desk in the corner. "This is yours. I despise clean desk policies, so keep your desk as you see fit as long as it's actually clean and anything on it is to do with work. You have a room upstairs, so you don't need personal items here."

The desk had a wooden top but was otherwise quite modern, and more to the point, it was raised to about chest height. It was a standing desk.

Susanna handed her a business card, "This is your username and password for the computer. You'll need to change the password, and I presume I don't need to tell you that you shouldn't write it down and leave it lying around? Candy and Sugar are little minxes, and if I find you've been subjected to their pranks, it will be you that is punished the most severely."

"Yes, Mistress," Amber nodded. "Are there password restrictions?"

"Yes, on the back of the card. Once you are logged in, you can use our password manager to handle other accounts you need access to. I think you have access to everything I need you to, but if not, let me know. I have an IT girl who can come and deal with any technical problems you might have."

"Thank you, Mistress."

"The desk is adjusted with these buttons. It's electric, so it's not hard. I assume you're familiar with how to correctly set up your desk for the best ergonomics but if not, look for an online guide. I cannot abide young ladies who make themselves unavailable because they don't look after their health," Susanna said with a somewhat testy tone, given that Amber herself hadn't made this particular mistake yet.

"I understand, Mistress. I'll make sure the desk is adjusted properly," Amber confirmed.

"Good. As you can see, it is a standing desk. I expect you to use it in the standing position unless I tell you otherwise. It promotes good health and strong legs. If you really cannot bear it, I may let you lower it for a while, but you'll soon learn to stand all day. For the Victorians, it was the norm you know," Susanna said as if the Victorians were somehow virtuous and to be diligently replicated in every thought and deed. Amber knew that despite any accomplishments they were also, by modern standards, a bunch of horrible buggers.

"Yes, Mistress," was all she said, though."

"Now, as to your work I have a simple series of tasks for you today, " Susanna continued. "They're all listed in the task management software on your PC. I am having a party next weekend which was organised before your references came through. There are some follow-up tasks for you to carry out, mostly to do with checking that everything is ready, sending out email reminders and the like. If you have any major problems, come into my office and speak to me. Otherwise, you can use the messaging system you'll find on your desktop so you don't interrupt my workflow. Questions?"

"Umm, no," Amber replied, "I think I have everything, Mistress."

"Really? I sense otherwise. Out with it girl, I don't have time for you to be coy," Susanna snapped.

"Well, it was just."

"Just what, spit it out for heaven's sake, Amber!"

Amber coughed, "Every day so far you've. Umm. You've enjoyed me. In the morning, after we woke up, but not today. Have I displeased you, Mistress?"

Susanna raised an eyebrow. "I see. You're upset that I haven't fucked you today?"

Amber blushed. "No. I don't mean. Not like that anyway. Umm. I mean, I was just surprised, is all," Amber stumbled, wilting somewhat under the exceptionally stern look Susanna was giving her. It felt like an industrial laser was aimed at the midpoint between her eyebrows.

Her Mistress didn't respond, she just turned and pulled open the double doors to her private office, "Come in, and shut the doors after yourself." Amber swiftly did as she was told.

"Stand there," Susanna said, motioning to a spot in front of her massive mahogany desk. Once Amber was in place, she slid into position behind her, reached around her, undid her belt and unbuttoned her jodhpurs. With a quick tug, Susanna pulled the tight trousers down below her bum.

"Bend over, place your forearms on the desk for support, either side of this cushion, and your forehead on the cushion. I don't want you getting a mark on your forehead," Susanna said, placing a small seat cushion on the edge of the desk.

Amber was thoroughly exposed once she had complied. Her buttocks were bare, and Susanna didn't take long to pull her lacy thong down to join her jodhpurs around her thighs, leaving her pussy lips open to viewing as well.

The fingertips that Susanna used to stroke her lips were soon slick with Amber's mounting excitement, and they plunged into her with barely any resistance. Amber gasped, despite the fact that Susanna's intrusion had been predictable once she was told to bend over like that.

In moments, Susanna had found her G-spot and was vigorously working it under her soft-skinned but unyielding fingers. Amber could barely contain her mounting pleasure, her quick breathing and low moans filled the office.

"Is this what you expected of me, slut?" Susanna growled.

Amber could only nod, unable to form words. "You think you're entitled to this sort of treatment, do you?"

Sensing a trap, Amber shook her head and regained enough composure to mumble, "No, Mistress."

"Liar. That's exactly what my kindness each day has led you to assume is your due. Are you close? Are you going to come soon?"

"Yes, Mistress," Amber groaned. The motion ceased, and Susanna's fingers withdrew from her aching pussy, only to be thrust rudely into her mouth.

"Suck them clean, slut," came the order which Amber greedily obeyed as her mounting arousal betrayed her and was routed from the field. Her breathing slowed as she sucked the musky fingers that Susanna had pushed into her mouth.

Then the fingers were entangled in her hair, and Amber found herself strongly encouraged to waddle around the desk, her legs still restricted by the jodhpurs around her thighs. "Kneel," Susanna ordered as undid her own belt and let her jodhpurs drop down to her knees.

Her Mistress sat down on the expensive office chair, parting her legs as much as the trousers would allow. The knee-length riding boots prevented them from dropping to her ankles. Amber found her face forced uncomfortably between Susanna's thighs where it was clamped in position. She was lucky that her nose was at a sufficient angle or she'd have been unable to breathe properly as she took up her duty.

"Look at me," Susanna snapped, as her thighs pressed against Amber's cheeks and her fist gripped her hair painfully. Amber looked up as best she could given the awkward position. "You do not determine when and where I play with you. You do not decide when I want to use your tongue or allow you pleasure. You most certainly do not make demands on my time. I am the one who decides, who determines, who demands. You are the submissive. You will do as you are told, or you will rue the day you disobeyed me. When you serve me well, I may grant you freedoms and pleasures you long for, but I will do so on my own advice. Comfortable down there?"

Amber could barely move her head, so firmly was she gripped, but she managed just enough to indicate that she was not. "Good!" Susanna remarked as she reached her orgasm and smeared her lips all over Amber's face, covering her in her arousal before letting go.

Amber winced as the pressure on her ears and the tug against her hair was relinquished, falling back gasping for air.

Susanna stood and patted herself down with a wipe she produced from her drawer. "Get up, slut. Go and wash your face and put your makeup in order, then come back ready to work hard."

Frustrated and filthy, Amber nevertheless did as she was told and retired to make herself look presentable again.

When she returned to the suite, the doors to Susanna's office were emphatically closed, and she got her head down and concentrated on the party planning tasks. Amber didn't dare disturb her Mistress further, not even with more apologies she felt compelled to give.

A couple of hours later, the doors opened, and Susanna emerged.

"Off to the races then," she said without another word on the morning's events.

Amber followed meekly, at the side of her Mistress but a half-step behind.

CHAPTER 2

The gravel of the courtyard crunched underfoot as they walked briskly toward the stables. There were quite a large number of outbuildings around the estate that Amber had seen, but many were in relative disrepair and seemingly unused.

When they approached the stable block though, it was clear the old brick building had been renovated in recent years. Amber couldn't date it, but the brick showed it's age, though it had clearly been repointed in recent years. More telling where the huge wooden doors, presumably designed for carriages. One wing had been converted into more modern garages, and Amber idly wondered what cars Susanna kept. No doubt, they were all expensive.

The building was at least two stories high, with a hayloft hatch and a winch at one end. Skylights in the opposite end of the roof suggested that section had been converted for office or living space in the loft area at least. They entered through a human-sized door at the end near the winch, but not under it. No-one wanted a hay bale dropped on their head when they were getting in or out. There were thick yellow lines under the winch, a nod to modern health and safety concerns which suggested it was still in use.

The internal proportions were quite cavernous, and Amber could immediately see several sections which were to hold large, four-horse carriages to their right, facing the courtyard the stables shared with the main house.

To the left were the stalls for the horses, the doors to them were split into two sections, with the lower one being slightly taller. The upper doors were open and held in place by a simple wooden latch. Above two of the stalls was a large, polished wooden sign bearing what Amber presumed was the name of the animal.

"Amber, why don't you introduce yourself to Pepper?" Susanna said, handing her two-quarters of a freshly sliced and juicy apple. "Give her a treat, and you'll soon win her over. Don't worry, she's not a biter. My ponies are very well trained. I'll be racing with Ginger today."

Amber took the apple and approached the stall. That they were ponies and not horses explained why she couldn't see their heads poking over the partial door. She still couldn't see the pony as she reached the door, but she heard a soft rustle of hay. Was it lying down?

"Go on in, my ponies are perfectly safe, Amber," Susanna said as she opened the door and stepped into Ginger's stall. "There you go, you silly creature, I've brought you a snack." There was a distinct crunch as the apple Susanna had was gobbled up.

Amber looked back at the door, lifted the latch and stepped into the stall. "I've got a treat for you, Pepper," she managed to get out before her eyes adjusted to the shadow. "Fuck me," she exclaimed under her breath.

Pepper stamped her foot softly but firmly and whinnied around the bit in her mouth. The hoof made a clopping sound against the floor of the stall, muffled by the hay.

Susanna's pony advanced on the dumbstruck personal assistant and dipped her head, using her lips to scoop up a chunk of apple and crunching it happily as Amber watched.

Living up to her name, Pepper had a fiery mane and a brightness to her eyes the spoke of intelligence and spirit. Her legs were long, elegant and firmly muscled. Her ears were pricked up and alert, and she was already prepared for racing it seemed, wearing a bridle and harness with a bit in her mouth. No sooner had she finished her first treat, than she dipped her head to snatch the second.

Amber simply looked the young woman up and down. Pepper was breathtaking to behold, a genuine beauty. The leather of her harness accentuated her lean body, which was a testament to her level of exercise and yet she'd retained delightful curves in all the places that Amber would have wished her too.

"Well," came the voice from the neighbouring stall, "what do you think of Pepper? She's a fine pony, isn't she?"

Amber cleared her throat. "I'm no expert, but she appears very fine to me indeed, and she looks ready to race her heart out." Pepper whinnied, and her eyes sparkled at Amber. She stamped her foot again twice in quick succession.

"That means yes, in case you were wondering," Susanna called out. "Lead her out of the front of the stall when you're done checking her out, and we'll get them hitched up to the traps."

"Yes, Mistress," Amber called out absently. Slowly she approached Pepper, and whispered, "You're beautiful, Pepper. May I… may I touch you?" Her question was slightly hesitant. She wasn't sure quite how to communicate with the ponygirl. Two quick soft stamps for yes were her answer though so Amber reached out and stroked the flank of the young woman who would be her pony for the day. Pepper's skin was smooth and chill in the stable air, but she didn't flinch away. She wasn't nervous.

Amber kept eye contact with her as she drew her hand up to the other woman's chest, cupping her breast and running a thumb over a nipple which grew rapidly erect. Pepper didn't seem to object to the attention at all. Her nipples were pierced with simple silver bars, held in place by balls at either end. Though she longed to place her mouth on Pepper's aroused breast, she guessed Susanna wasn't going to allow her more than a brief time to admire her pony before she wanted to race them.

Reluctantly, Amber took up the reins and unlatched the door that led into a small grassy area, ringed in by a fence. Susanna was almost done getting Ginger into position with a small, one person trap. When she was done, she came over to see how Amber was progressing.

Amber looked at her helplessly, "I'm really not sure what to do here."

Susanna smiled. "We're just here to have fun, Amber. Ginger and Pepper need regular exercise and play to keep them fit, healthy and happy. Here, let me show you how you harness them to the trap, so they're safe and comfortable."

True to her word, Susanna showed her once, then removed Pepper from the trap and made Amber do it herself, once with pointers and the second time on her own. It wasn't complicated, but Susanna was very careful to stress all the safety protocols to avoid injury.

"Now, check that her tail is nicely in place, we don't want it to fall out."

Amber crouched behind Pepper and inspected the swishy tail. It was attached to a butt plug that was plunged into Pepper's bottom. Moving the hair aside, she made a show of inspecting it. First, she applied a little pressure to check if it was fully inserted, then she attempted to withdraw it, and move it left to right. Pepper made soft whinnying sounds as she did so, but the plug stayed firmly in her arse.

"It seems secure, Mistress."

"Excellent. Now, the last check is to ensure your pony is hot to trot as it were," Susanna said, demonstrating as she reached between Ginger's thighs and got a strong whinny and foot stamp from her. "Like so."

Amber followed suit, "Are you going to win this race for me, Pepper?" The woman's pussy was invitingly wet with her arousal, swallowing Amber's fingers with ease. Peper's eyes flashed, and she stamped her foot twice quickly as Amber whispered encouragement.

Turning back to Susanna, Amber held up her fingers, glistening with Pepper's juices. She slid them into her mouth and sucked them clean. "I think Pepper is more than hot to trot, Mistress."

Susanna laughed. "It's around the lake once. The ponies know the route, and I suggest only light encouragement with your carriage whip until you know what you're doing. Across the buttocks only. Do a slow circuit of the paddock so you can get used to it and then we'll go down to the lake."

Amber nodded her understanding as she climbed into the light-weight trap and Pepper took up the handles, tilting it back and moving off at a slow walk.

"The prize is an orgasm," Susanna called out as they set off down to the small lake.

"I'll take that bet, Mistress," Amber replied boldly.

CHAPTER 3

"**P**ick up the pace, Ginger!" Susanna cried as she cracked the whip in the air above her. Ginger was probably doing her best, Amber thought. There was no way she was going to be able to catch up with Pepper now though.

They were already in sight of the fork in the track they'd started the race at, and Pepper showed no signs of flagging. The lake wasn't enormous but pulling a trap with a person in it around a rather rudimentary track wasn't that easy. Amber could easily see why Pepper's thighs were so impressively muscled, strong and lean if she was regularly pulling Susanna around this track.

"You too, Pepper!" Amber said, cracking her own whip. Pepper neighed, but when Amber finished her practice sweeps and let the whip contact first her left and then her right buttock, she squealed past her gag.

Her pony stumbled, and Amber thought she might stop entirely, but after a moment, she collected herself and ran on, gradually increasing her space. Pepper pulled over the finish line with at least a hundred yards between her and her rival ponygirl. The trap came to a slow halt as Pepper's pace slowed and she finally halted.

Amber could hear the ponygirl gulping in big lungfuls of air. She'd really pushed herself for her driver, and her flanks were covered in sweat.

Susanna and Ginger pulled up alongside them, and her Mistress dismounted, coming over to Amber's trap. "Well done, you beat us, fair and square."

"Thank you, Mistress."

"How did you manage that, when you've never raced a ponygirl before, hmm?"

"Beginner's luck, Mistress," Amber demurred.

"Really? I notice you gave her a couple of good marks here, " Susanna said, running her hand over Pepper's bottom, feeling the bruised scarlet flesh. "That's an astonishing learning curve you've got there. They're just right. These look lovely, Pepper." The ponygirl whinnied appreciatively.

Amber got down from her trap and Pepper was finally able to relax, squatting down to carefully put the arms of the single-person trap down. She stood on the other side of Pepper and reached out, stroking the ponygirl's welted skin. Had she really caused that? Pepper yelped and turned her head to give her a reproachful look.

"I think Pepper thinks she was going to win without the added inducement," Susanna said, walking around the girl to whisper in Amber's ear. "You should get out of the trap and check your ponygirl as soon as you finish, to make sure they're ok. Now, check to see if she's responding as you'd hope to the welts you gave her."

Amber wasn't sure what her Mistress meant by that and Susanna raised an eyebrow at her before nodding an acknowledgement that her protege was confused. Mistress took hold of her right hand and guided her to Pepper's flank, sliding Amber's fingers over the moist skin and down between her thighs.

Susanna's breath was hot against her ear as she whispered, "Is she wet? Excited? Aroused? Does she lust for the touch of your fingers or the kiss of your whip?" Her teeth nibbled gently at Amber's earlobe, and her lips drew together around it to bring gentle suction to her.

With her fingers between Pepper's legs, she explored the ponygirl's smoothly shaved sex. Her lips were as wet as her perspiration drenched chest. Pepper shuddered and gamely attempted to whinny, but it came out as half a moan, and it was all Amber could do not to giggle.

"Guide her head by her mane, let her see you taste her arousal," Susanna whispered.

Amber reached out and took hold of Pepper's hair, which was plaited in a long tail. Of course, it was. She made the girl look at her and smiled as she lifted her fingers from their exploration of Pepper's pussy and sucked them clean. Pepper's eyes flashed with fire, and Amber grinned.

Their Mistress came forward then and looked at Pepper seriously. "Now, Pepper. Did Amber really win because she had beginner's luck?" Pepper tossed her head from side to side, giving a remarkably negative sounding neigh and stamping her foot three times for no. Amber cursed inside.

"Amber, remove her bit gag, please," Susanna ordered her, waiting for the rubber bar to be unstrapped from the ponygirl's face.

"Pepper, you may speak. Tell me how Amber won," Susanna demanded. The ponygirl glanced at Amber and then shook her head and stamped her foot three times. Amber's eyes widened. This surely wasn't going to go well for Pepper. She was risking the wrath of their Mistress.

"Come along then girls, we're going back to the stables," Mistress Susanna said finally, having glared at the pair of them. She led Ginger away, walking beside her holding her reins and Amber followed suit, beside Pepper.

The walk from the lakeside back to the stables didn't take long but all the way Amber wondered what would happen next as traipsed through the grass.

They put the traps away, and the girl's bits and bridles were cleaned in a large butler's sink, dried down and hung up in the tack room. Susanna then took them to a room that bore a brass plaque which read, "Training and Discipline".

"Amber, strap Pepper down over that punishment bench, and make sure she's properly restrained," Susanna ordered, pointing at a piece of furniture. The punishment bench resembled a gymnastics vaulting horse that had been crossed with a piece of modern gym equipment. It was padded and covered with glossy black leather, and festooned with buckles, rings, belts and straps clearly intended to restrain a human.

At first glance, Amber wasn't entirely sure she was interpreting the design correctly, but she breathed a mental sigh of relief when Pepper meekly mounted the bench. As the ponygirl got into position, Amber's understanding of how the bench was intended to be used proved remarkably accurate. A long pad either side of the body of the bench provided a place for the submissive's knees and another pair further along the bench allowed Pepper to rest her forearms.

Rather than being flat though, the knee and forearm rests were below the height of the bench, and so Pepper was held in position as if she was on all fours, with her torso supported. There was a subtle incline to the bench, so her head was slightly lower down than her buttocks.

Amber set about using the thick leather cuffs to restrain Pepper's wrists and ankles, before adding the straps which restrained her near the elbows and knees as well. Pepper whinnied and struggled against the restraints, proving that she couldn't free herself. Amber looked at her boss, who had mounted a wooden platform which raised the wooden throne she now occupied, above the floor by a good few inches.

Her boss, scrutinised her work, finally nodding, "Is she ready for punishment, Amber?" she asked. As she spoke, she casually ran her fingers through the hair of her pony, Ginger, who was kneeling beside the throne of her Mistress.

"Yes, Mistress," Amber replied, hoping that she hadn't missed any restraints.

"Is her tail still secure?" Susanna asked.

Amber reached out and took hold of the tail that sprouted from Pepper's pert bottom, near the root where the long hairs were attached to the silicon butt plug that filled the ponygirls arse. She tugged at it gently, finding the plug was still held firmly and wasn't going to come loose with a light pull. Pepper shuddered and groaned as the plug insert in her bottom was wiggled from side to side.

"Pepper's tail is secure, Mistress," Amber reported.

"Are the lips of her sex wet?"

Amber stepped to the side and bent at the waist to get a better look, "I think so, Mistress."

Susanna shook her head. "Not good enough. Kneel behind her, Amber. Use your tongue to confirm Pepper's state."

Amber obliged her Mistress without complaint, it was hardly a chore to use her tongue on the comely ponygirl, after all. Pepper was indeed wet before Amber's tongue slipped between then the lips of her pussy, and began lapping at her. She wondered how long she was supposed to do this before updating her Mistress, trying to glance to the side as she ate Pepper's pussy, but finding her Mistress's throne was positioned to the left of her, but also just far enough behind her that she couldn't see her without leaving her assigned task to turn a bit.

"Well? Is she fully aroused?" Susanna asked.

Amber pulled back and turned at the waist to face Mistress Susanna. "Yes, Mistress. I can confirm Pepper is in a clear state of arousal. Her lips are wet and delicious."

"Good, then she is ready to be punished. Stand up and come here."

"Yes, Mistress."

"Now, with which implements should Pepper be punished, hmm?"

Amber shrugged. "I'm not sure, Mistress. Which would you prefer?"

"Are you not, Amber? You must learn to make such choices on your own, and this seems like a good opportunity for you to practice your skills. Her punishment is due to be delivered, and you will give it, won't you, Amber?" Susanna replied.

Amber bowed her head, nodding agreement, "Yes, Mistress. As you wish."

"That's right. Pepper failed to truthfully answer my question, and now I expect you to induce her to do so. Do you think you can do that?"

If Pepper confessed how Amber had won and what she had promised the ponygirl, Amber knew her inducement would be revealed to their Mistress, and it seemed likely she'd be punished as well. On the other hand, if she failed to extract the truth from her, Amber could picture the situation being reversed. It would be Amber who was strapped to the bench and Pepper would be the one punisher her to correct her cunning behaviour.

It was a classic situation of being caught between a spanking bench and a hard paddle, Amber knew. Whatever she did, would likely result in punishment for her and Pepper both.

Amber swallowed hard and did her best to sound upbeat when she replied, "I'm sure that with your expert tutelage, Mistress, I could extract the truth you require from your submissive."

"This is a test for you, Amber, so I shall only guide you if I feel it is strictly necessary to do so," Susanna said. Gesturing to a rack of implements, she asked, "These are your tools. Which do you think will elicit the truth most expeditiously. Make your choice and begin Pepper's punishment. Quickly girl."

Amber hurried across the room and began to investigate the rack of impact play equipment that her Mistress had indicated. It was a beautifully crafted wooden rack, with abundant slots, hooks and rests for a wide variety of items that would thrill any sadist to use or any masochist to be the recipient of.

Honestly, she felt spoilt for choice. There were canes, small floggers, elegant carriage whips, a handful of tawses, several wooden rules of desk and classroom length, a selection of paddles made of wood or leather, or sometimes both. Some had words stitched into them or metal studs on one side.

Amber rejected the riding crops and the floggers, which she imagined Pepper would be able to tolerate quite admirably. Instead, she imagined how she might feel and the things that Susanna had already done to her. What would make her resistance to questioning crumble, and her secrets spill from her lips?

The tawse seemed likely to provide an impact that would soon bring Pepper to the point that she could no longer bear to stay silent.

Amber knew it must be painful as Susanna had offered Sugar and Candy the chance to torment her with a tawse or a school cane if she had failed a challenge. She had won, so hadn't yet experienced the tawse for herself, as such she wasn't sure it was wise to apply it to Pepper's beautiful cheeks.

Chewing her lip and sensing a growing impatience from her Mistress, Amber made her choice. She took hold of a handle and slowly withdrew a long, bamboo cane with a curved handle. This was no rough cane such as a gardener might use to support a plant, but a carefully selected and shaped tool of corporal punishment. It was thick enough to impact her palm audibly when she swished it down into her left hand but thin enough to sting.

Amber gave it a few practice swishes, like a youngster playing with a wooden sword, and it made an evil noise as it cut through the air. Pepper performed her part admirably, whinnying and testing her restraints as if she was afraid of the cane.

"Begin!" Susanna snapped, clearly impatient to watch Amber work.

The first stroke landed on Pepper's buttocks, lower than Amber had meant it to, a few seconds later. It was harder than she had intended and the line it scored just above the creases where Pepper's buttocks met her thighs, was close to scarlet.

Pepper's response was audible and shrill, but Amber knew better than to panic by now. Amber carefully lined up her next shot, and this time, her aim was true. The cane landed across both buttocks, causing another yelp from Pepper which was far more human than pony-like and a less lurid mark appeared.

Concentrating hard, Amber began to count out strokes of the cane, since Pepper was a pony and couldn't very well count them aloud for the woman who was dominating her, at the behest of their Mistress.

With each stroke, she struggled to maintain an even tempo, amount of force and keep her aim in check. The lines she left across the pony's buttocks crossed more often than Amber wanted them to, but she soon found herself able to distribute them down toward Pepper's thighs and up toward her back. They weren't perfectly parallel stripes as she imagined she wanted them to be, but she was rather chuffed that she didn't land any more strokes too far down or above the area, she was trying to aim for.

Amber would have liked to deliver a pattern that resembled lined paper for handwriting in terms of spacing and neatness. She felt a sense of achievement that her lines were as they were, but they crossed one another and made more of a deep pink rectangular splotch than a precisely lined up series of marks.

The effect on the previously pristine flesh of the young submissive's shapely bottom was wonderfully appealing. Amber wondered what that bottom would look like if she could divide it up with neat perpendicular stripes and hoped she'd one day get to find out. As her own feelings of satisfaction and arousal from submitting to Susanna deepened, she was also finding the thought of disciplining other young women, increasingly appealing.

By the time she was at fifteen strokes, it was apparent that Susanna wasn't going to stop her at some traditional number such as six of the best or a dozen hard strokes. She sensed that if she kept the strokes as they were, she could thoroughly redden Pepper's cheeks, without raising prominent welts. Reaching out, she confirmed that Pepper's bottom was as hot as the glowing skin seemed to suggest. Pepper shuddered at her touch.

"Will you talk, Pepper?" Amber asked, hopefully.

Pepper tossed her mane from side to side, refusing to break character.

Amber smiled to herself and licked her lips. For Pepper's sake, she knew the ponygirl should talk. But the act of punishing her was making her wet, even though she anticipated that breaking the girl would most likely result in her own punishment.

If Pepper had agreed to answer right then, she would not be able to deliver the next strokes of the cane, which had the girl whimpering in a most human fashion. As it was, she continued to discipline the stalwart ponygirl, with hard, even strokes. Amber found her brow creased as she concentrated intently on landing each stroke as close to her target as possible.

Pepper was vocally but wordlessly protesting each time the thing length of bamboo left an impression on her prominently displayed cheeks. Although she was stood to one side of the submissive, Amber could still see the telltale moisture on her lips that made them glisten enticingly even as the caning reddened her cheeks.

The state of her pussy was reliable confirmation of Pepper's continued state of arousal. Likewise, her breathing matched the pattern of a woman in a state of arousal, rather than in discomfort. While Pepper didn't sound close to orgasm, Amber was sure that Pudding would have been able to produce that result from the ponygirl, with the application of discipline. Pepper clearly had a taste for such games.

Mistress Susanna stood up and made her way to the other side of the bench, watching Amber's progress as she beat the unfortunate ponygirl.

"Your accuracy is coming along nicely, Amber. I don't think Pepper here is going to give in when you are pulling your strikes as much as you are though. Why don't you bring it up a notch, eh? Lay it on a little harder, see if you can bring tears to her eyes, hmm?" Susanna advised.

Pepper thrashed uselessly at her bindings, but Amber planted her left hand firmly at the base of her spine and held the wriggling submissive in place. The ponygirl was powerless to resist. The only way she could get out of this was to break character as a pony and beg for mercy as a human.

"Yes, Mistress. As you command," Amber said. She chewed her lip as she took aim once more and let rip with six strokes of the cane.

Pepper howled, and Ginger gasped in shock. Then Pepper gamely whinnied again, and Amber knew she hadn't won yet. Susanna nodded at her, and Amber continued with the punishment at the new level encouraged by her boss. Pepper took it well, Amber thought, indeed, despite the audible distress she gave voice to, her buttocks shifted, straining up to meet the kiss of Amber's bamboo. The slut was enjoying her own suffering. Pepper wasn't merely aroused, she was eager for more.

Amber was only too happy to oblige. She would not have thought it even a fortnight ago, but the act of disciplining this willing young woman was intensely satisfying to her. She wished she had another submissive kneeling before her right now, worshipping her pussy with a slippery tongue as she caned Pepper.

"You will answer, Mistress Susanna, Pepper, or I swear you will be unable to sit for a week," Amber boasted.

Pepper shook her head slowly, and Susanna smiled as Amber altered her aim and landed the next six stripes just below her target area. The fresh patch of skin was barely marked from the occasional errant stroke, and by the fifth landing on the sensitive area, Pepper had tears streaming freely down her cheeks.

Susanna moved to the head of the punishment horse and took a firm grip of Pepper's mane of hair, plaited to resemble a pony, as was only fitting. The Mistress of the house crouched a little, tilting her submissive's head back and up, and locking eyes with her even as Amber continued to cane her.

"Will you talk now, Pepper? Reveal your secrets, and this punishment will end. You don't have to suffer like this. You have stayed in character well, my dear, and I am very proud of you for doing so. It thrills me to watch you suffer for me like this, to bravely play your role as a ponygirl and refuse to talk. And yet I think you are close to the edge and must talk soon, no?" Susanna asked.

Pepper tried to shake her head but nodded slightly, finally appearing to give in. Amber stopped, and Susanna raised an eyebrow. "I didn't tell you to stop caning this slut, did I, Amber? Continue until I tell you otherwise. Pepper, stick your bottom up as high as you can for Amber, there's a good girl."

Pepper gave a throaty whimper of anguish but obediently did as she was told and Amber marvelled at the control that Susanna had over her. The ponygirl presented her tormented cheeks as best she could, a most enticing target for her to discipline. Once she had, Amber did as her Mistress commanded as well.

"Did you make an extra effort to win the race for Amber, Pepper?"

"Yes, Mistress," the ponygirl cried out between sobs and strokes of Amber's cane.

"Did she ask you to do so?"

"Yes, Mistress."

"Did you she offer you some kind of bribe or inducement to outshine Ginger?" Susanna asked.

"Yes, Mistress she did."

"What did she promise you?" Susanna said, smiling as Amber's cane elicited another wail of shock from Pepper.

"She… she promised me pleasure, Mistress. She promised to sneak out one night and bring me off with her tongue if I could beat Ginger," Pepper wailed.

"Did she now? Is this true, Amber?" Susanna asked.

"Yes, Mistress."

Susanna stood up and clapped her hands triumphantly. "Excellent, you may stop disciplining her now, Amber. About your choice of implement…" Susanna began.

"Yes, Mistress?" Amber asked.

"You chose… wisely."

"Thank you, Mistress," Amber said, gratefully returning the cane to the rack after wiping it down with a cloth.

"Now, help my reposition the bench," Susanna demanded. Together, she and Amber turned the bench ninety degrees so that Pepper was facing the throne.

Once she was happy with the new positioning, Susanna alighted her throne again, slouching a little so that she could spread her knees apart. Beckoning to Ginger, she casually gave her an order, "Loosen my jodhpurs and lick me to orgasm, Ginger."

The ponygirl did just that with practised ease and a lustful grin in her eyes. She sighed contentedly as her tongue worked between her lips.

"Isn't she a good girl, Amber?" Susanna asked as Ginger tongued her vigorously.

"Yes, Mistress. I'm sure all the ladies you choose soon learn to be good girls," Amber replied.

"In most cases, that is true. Some still seek to defy me or by cheeky though, don't they, Amber?"

"No doubt, Mistress."

"Speaking of which, you may make up for your borderline unsportsmanlike behaviour by removing your clothing and laying down with your head under Ginger's hips. I'm sure Ginger would like an orgasm from your wicked tongue, and Pepper will learn a lesson from watching her receive the pleasure she was promised, don't you think?" Susanna said.

Amber nodded and began to strip. "As you wish, Mistress."

Ginger lifted her head for a fraction of a second to add, "Yes, Mistress. Thank you, Mistress."

Pepper did not speak.

Within moments the tableau was set. Mistress Susanna reigned on her throne, while her ponygirl Ginger gleefully licked her pussy for all she was worth. Amber lay on her back, while Ginger's hips were lowered until she was almost sitting on her face, and her tongue was buried in the young submissive's pussy.

Susanna ordered Amber to improve the show for the still bound Pepper, by spreading her knees apart and playing with her own pussy. Unlike Ginger, however, she was denied the satisfaction of her own orgasm and threatened with most harsh punishments if she did cum without the permission of her Mistress.

Poor Pepper had merely to look on while Amber rode the waves of each orgasm, almost to the peak before their Mistress ruined it with a harsh word or a flick of her carriage whip, skillfully skirting over Ginger's buttocks, to sting Amber's thighs.

Amber could hear the muffled screams she gave at this, even as her eyes stung with salty tears and her tongue worked hard at Ginger's delicious lips.

Although Pepper and Amber had won the race, Ginger and Mistress Susanna felt the most satisfaction at the end of their ponygirl session.

When finally their Mistress was satiated, she showed Amber how to hose down the ponygirls, in a shower room specially set up for them, then towel them off and send back to their stalls.

With Amber still entirely nude, they made their way back to the house, the assistant following a half-step behind her imperious boss, in awe of the older woman who now controlled her life.

"Mistress, may I ask about Ginger and Pepper?"

"Ask what?"

Taking that response as implied permission, Amber pushed on. "When we got to the stables, they were already dressed up. Do they spend all their time like that?"

"Hmm. Do you mean 24 hours a day, 7 days a week? No. I know some people who find that a thrill but we experimented with their roleplaying as ponygirls and settled on a system that satisfies us all. I have a buzzer I can ring from the house that notifies them when I'm visiting, and a clock can give them a countdown if need be. That way they can get in character before I arrive," Susanna replied.

"Who dresses them up?"

"They dress each other."

"Can I ask what they do when you aren't here to play with them? What do they do when you're in the City, or you just don't have the time or inclination?"

Susanna stopped and turned to face Amber. "They have their own work to do, Amber. Just as you do. They keep the stables in order, obviously but they both have graphic and web design skills they use to support my companies. There is a bedroom they share above the stables, well, a small flat with a bathroom and kitchen and the work from there. Anything else?"

"No, Mistress. Thank you for explaining it," Amber said, then paused for a moment. She cocked her head and went on, "Except. Do they wait for you for all their pleasure, or do they play with each other or Candy and Sugar, Mistress?"

Her boss sighed dramatically, and in a blur of motion, she moved in close with Amber, causing her to backpedal swiftly until she found herself pushed up against a wall that she thought belonged to the kitchen garden.

Susanna halted any further conversation with a deep, possessive kiss, her tongue slipping between Amber's lips. Her Mistress gripped her wrists and moved Amber's arms above her head, as she claimed her mouth. Her jodhpurs and blouse felt rough against Amber's naked skin as Susanna made it clear she was in charge.

Amber felt like a toy or a doll, posed and played with, as Susanna captured both her crossed wrists with her strong right hand, continuing to passionately lay kisses over her neck and breasts.

Without speaking, Susanna stroked her left hand over Amber's breasts, stroking and pinching her nipples, then ran it down between them, over her firm belly and between her legs. The questing fingers of her Mistress soon buried themselves between her wet lips and Amber gasped loudly as she felt her body respond.

It was mere moments before Susanna had drawn an explosive orgasm from Amber, one that left her panting hard with the heat and swiftness of the act. As quickly as her boss had taken control of her, she let go of Amber's wrists, and the young assistant sank to her knees in a post-orgasmic daze.

Susanna roughly grabbed her hair, and tilted her head up, staring down at Amber with her most imperious expression. "You all await my pleasure. Every hour, of every day. Ponygirls, maids, cooks and personal assistants. You serve my whims, cook my food, provide my pleasures and endure my discipline. All for the chance to please your Mistress. Do you know why?"

"No, Mistress," Amber breathed.

"Because your lusts run parallel to my own and it excites you to find out when they will next intersect. You all want my attention, my permission to behave as you do, you crave my orders to use your tongues and fingers to please each other, don't you, Amber?"

"Yes."

"Did it thrill you when I made you eat Ginger's pussy?"

"Yes."

"Make you wet when you caned Pepper?"

"Yes."

"Shock you when I pushed you against that wall?"

"Yes."

"Excite you when I thrust my fingers into your pussy and took you roughly?"

"Yes, Mistress."

Susanna hauled her back to her feet by her hair and Amber winced, as she was held against the wall again. "Do you think Ginger and Pepper play with each other while I am not present?" she asked in a throaty whisper, her cheek pressed against Amber's and her breath hot on her ear.

Amber shook her head, cautiously, "No, Mistress."

"No?"

Amber reconsidered. "Not unless you order it, Mistress. They are here to serve at your pleasure."

"Good answer," Susanna said. "Do you intend to go through with your promise to sneak out and pleasure Pepper?"

Swallowing hard, Amber shook her head. "No, Mistress."

"Why not?"

"Because I serve your pleasure, not hers," Amber answered hopefully, "or mine."

"Hah," Susanna scoffed. "Do you really, minx?"

"Yes, Mistress," Amber claimed.

"That's right. You do. You're lucky I don't punish you properly for making a promise you aren't entitled to keep, minx," Susanna growled.

"Yes, Mistress. I'm sorry, Mistress. I won't do it again," Amber promised.

Susanna laughed. "I don't believe all that, but if you do, I won't likely give you a free pass again. You understand what I'm saying?"

Amber nodded. "If I promise things like that again, you'll punish me, spanking me so hard I'll come from that alone and then make me lick your pussy for hours to apologise."

At that, Susanna chuckled. "I'm not sure how much of a punishment that would be for you, Amber but I'll bear your idea in mind."

"Yes, Mistress."

"As for your promise today, I expect you to honour it, of course."

Amber nodded but didn't speak, waiting for her Mistress to clarify her instruction, as she sensed she would.

"You will go to the stables tomorrow night, after I have finished with you, and spend the rest of the night pleasuring Pepper and Ginger in the way they see fit. You will submit to them as if they were me, and if they wish, they may punish you. I expect you will have an uncomfortable and exhausting night satisfying those two and they'll use you like the slut you so clearly are until none of you can stay awake. What do you say to that, Amber?" Susanna asked, one eyebrow raised in anticipation of a cheeky response.

Amber licked her lips and dropped to her knees before her Mistress, bowing her head until her forehead almost touched the ground. "I serve at the pleasure of my Mistress. Always and with pride," she said.

"As it should be."

CHAPTER 4

"Show me what you've done so far," Susanna said, looking over Amber's shoulder at her monitors.

"I've been working through the guest list and checking which ones have confirmed," Amber replied, demonstrating on the screen that she'd been ticking off the responses.

"Has everyone responded to the original invitation?"

"No, Mistress. These ones I've highlighted in yellow haven't replied yet that I can find."

"Six is too many, compose an email to them, and show it to me to check it before you send it. Ask them to respond by the end of the day tomorrow. If anyone still hasn't responded, we'll phone them, and I'll speak to them in person."

"Yes, Mistress. I should be done with this shortly. What should I do next?"

"Check on the deliveries we're expecting, if it's been shipped to us, confirm it's arrived. If it's arriving on the day, call the supplier and check if there are any problems. I've had too many soirees fall flat because the champagne or chocolate coated strawberries or cake didn't arrive," Susanna said.

Amber made notes as her boss talked and then glanced up at her to see if anything else was coming. Susanna had the off-centre gaze of someone who was sifting through their mind trying to remember something, so she waited patiently.

"Also, check up on Pudding. She's not doing all the catering, but she might need ingredients, or fresh produce or something. For the party to go well, it's crucial that Pudding is in a good mood and not feeling the effects of stress. She does fret so, and if there's a problem, she won't ask for help until she's failed to solve it, which just leads to whole stress. Then it becomes a thing. And I hate things," Susanna said, visibly shuddering at the thought of it. Amber bit her lip and turned her face away to hide her amusement.

With a little cough, she squeaked a reply, "Yes, Mistress."

"Good, let me know if you have any questions."

Amber nodded and began checking for responses from the guests as Susanna returned to her office.

It took less than an hour to confirm that almost everyone invited had already responded. A few noted special requirements such as dietary restrictions or allergies they wanted to notify them of. Fortunately, most were minor, but Amber made sure to take special note of the potentially dangerous allergies so that she could check the menu for peanuts and the like.

The email to ask the three outstanding guests if they could confirm whether or not they would be attending the weekend took a little longer. Amber wasn't quite sure how to approach it. It seems Mistress Susanna wanted these people to come to the event and expected that they would, but the fact they hadn't responded suggested they weren't the most organised of friends or colleagues.

Since Amber didn't know the purpose of the party, she wasn't sure if it was a business problem or a social problem if these people didn't come. Either way, she drafted and redrafted the email several times, trying to strike a balance between asking and insisting that the guests respond. Eventually, she had to send it to Susanna to be checked and hope she'd done an excellent job.

Once she had done that she began to go through the list of orders that Susanna had given her. Alcohol and soft drinks certainly weren't going to be a problem. Amber sincerely hoped that her boss was restocking the mansion's pantry because these deliveries contained enough booze to render the entire guest list insensible.

Given the number of people on the list whose names bore such formal honorifics as Lady, Dame and Madam, Amber didn't think they were going to have an undignified weekend of drunken debauchery. All she could really glean from the guest list was that they were all-powerful women, and they were bringing one or two people with them. Those people were only identified by an initial and their surname. They could be staff or family members or spouses for all Amber knew.

There wasn't time for her to dig into their backgrounds online and see if she could identify anyone though, and for the tasks she'd been given, it didn't matter anyway. Regardless of this being a business or a social event, Amber needed to do her best to ensure it went off without a hitch.

Her boss, Susanna, might tolerate a small problem, but Mistress Susanna would exact her revenge for sure if anything went wrong because of a mistake Amber made. Just the thought of what that would entail for such a public failure, made Amber squirm uncomfortably in her expensive office chair. She shook her head to clear it of diverting thoughts and got back to work.

Amber had made a couple of preemptive phone calls to suppliers before a notification popped up that Susanna had replied to her email. The response was brief, a couple of minor tweaks her boss requested and Amber was ready to send it. She filled in the recipient's email addresses and sent the mail.

Then it was time to finish off the supplier checks, which didn't take long. Finally, she was ready to tick off the last task on her list, and there was plenty of time before the end of a typical working day.

Amber stood up and stretched her back and neck.

Then with a cheerful grin, she went to the kitchen to speak to Pudding.

"Five bags of self-raising flour?"

"Umm. Yes, we've got those."

"Three bags of raisins and two of sultanas?" Pudding asked, crossing out the flour.

"Yes," Amber replied, pulling them out of the box the groceries had been delivered in.

"Wonderful. That's everything I needed then," Pudding said a little gruffly.

"It seems so. Is there anything else I can do to help?"

Pudding sighed. "No, not unless you're a qualified sous chef."

Amber laughed. "No, I'm afraid not. Anything that doesn't involve cooking?"

"No I'm just anxious about the event," Pudding said, looking up at Amber, "Mistress Susanna's parties always make me tense. I can't help worrying that I might get something wrong and ruin the event."

"Maybe a shoulder rub if you're feeling tense?" Amber suggested.

Pudding shook her head. "That doesn't work with me. I don't think Mistress sent you here to give me the kind of stress relief I enjoy."

Amber giggled. "I think she wants you to be relaxed for the weekend. Maybe she wouldn't mind if I gave you some pleasure."

"It sounds more like you want to put that wicked tongue of yours to good use than you want to help me," Pudding said. "That isn't my favourite way to relax anyway."

"No? I thought that relaxed everyone," Amber teased.

"It does, I suppose. But what really helps me find peace is a nice pair of rosy cheeks and a pretty girl bawling her eyes out over my lap."

"You'd find it more relaxing to just spank me?" Amber asked incredulously.

Pudding laughed at that. "Oh, after the spanking, the oral sex. I wouldn't let an opportunity to press my lips to your sweet mouth pass me by."

"You do seem awfully stressed about the party, perhaps you should ask Mistress to borrow me?" Amber said with a giggle.

Pudding cocked her head and stood up, beckoning to Amber,

"Alright minx, come with me." She led Amber into her suite and picked up a phone, dialling the intercom.

Amber found her chest tightening in anticipation. In truth she'd just been teasing Pudding, intending to report back to her boss that the cook wasn't in the best of moods. She hadn't meant to volunteer for a vigorous spanking to finish off her workday.

It came as no surprise when Pudding said, "Mistress, I wondered if I might beg the use of Amber for a while?"

Pudding nodded and passed the phone handset to Amber with an anticipatory gleam in her eye, "Mistress wants a word."

"Mistress?"

"Amber, what have you been up to?"

"Just doing as you asked and checking that Pudding has everything she needs for the weekend, Mistress," Amber replied.

"And does she?"

"No, I don't think so," Amber said.

"Does she want to spank you? Good and hard?"

"Yes, Mistress."

"I'm sure she'd put your tongue to good use after that," Susanna replied, "while the tears streamed down your cheeks, I imagine."

"I believe that is her plan, Mistress."

"Does the prospect excite you, Amber?" Susanna asked.

"Yes, Mistress, it does," Amber admitted.

"I see, then who am I to stand in the way of Pudding getting some much-needed stress relief. You'll do as she says. I want you back up here at a quarter to five at the latest though," Susanna said, "now pass the phone back to Pudding, there's a good little slut."

Amber handed the phone over to Pudding whose face lit up as she listened to their Mistress.

"Thank you, Mistress. I'm sure I'll feel much more relaxed about the weekend soon," Pudding said. The cook listened to the response and then obediently replied, "Yes, of course. As you wish, Mistress."

Pudding put the phone down but not in the cradle. The cook wasn't hanging up, she just rested the handset on the desk, the line for Mistress Susanna's office was still open so she could hear everything. Amber considered that, chewing her lip for a moment, while Pudding watched her.

"Are you ready, Amber?" Pudding finally asked.

"Yes, Pudding."

"Then why don't you take off all your clothes so I can appreciate your beautiful young body."

Amber nodded and began slowly, teasingly, stripping off her clothes.

Pudding shook her head, "No, don't flirt with me. I want you naked now."

"Yes, Pudding," Amber said, hurrying her unbuttoning up. She was nude and turning slowly at Puddings command in a few moments, showing off her body for the cook.

"You are a beautiful young woman, Amber. I'm going to enjoy you. Thank you for volunteering to help me wind down. I suppose that might make another woman go easy on you, but I will be looking to see your cheeks moist with tears," Pudding said. "I enjoy spanking a younger woman, but I simply adore hearing them weeping and wailing. It's so exciting. If you want a shred of comfort in that, perhaps it would help to be reminded that my preferred instrument is my own palm and not a cane or whip. Now, why don't you come here and put yourself over my knee so I can begin?"

Amber bent herself over Pudding's lap, her knees resting on the velvet upholstery of the chaise longue Pudding favoured. There was no preamble, beyond what Pudding had already said. She simply began to spank Amber, and she didn't offer the young woman any build up from a light smack to a fierce impact.

Instead, Pudding went straight for a hard spanking from the first. Her left hand was in the small of Amber's back, holding her in place even before Pudding's right hand made Amber cry out in pain and begin to wriggle.

"You can struggle if you want, Amber but I'm not letting go. If it were really too much for you, you'd use your safeword," Pudding stated flatly.

When the prospect of getting a spanking this late in the afternoon had first been mooted, Amber had imagined a long session of carefully progressive impact play, building her slowly toward a climactic outpouring of tears. Instead, she could immediately feel her eyes watering. Pudding was taking her frustrations out on her bottom, and she could picture it in her mind's eye, glowing hot and deep red.

Her cheeks were warming up rapidly, and Pudding was setting a fearsome tempo, like a metronome set to a hundred beats per minute. The thought made Amber let forth an involuntary giggle, which was immediately interrupted by the next smack.

"Do you think this is funny?" Pudding demanded, "You offered yourself up for a spanking, and you're getting a good firm going over, and you find something amusing in this?"

Amber gasped, as Pudding stopped for a moment, taking a firm grip on her hair and tilting her head up. "Well? Answer me, girl!" the cook demanded.

"No, Pudding. It's not funny."

"Then, why did you laugh?" Pudding demanded, punctuating each word with another smack.

"I'm sorry," Amber managed. "Your spanks are so fast and rhythmical I couldn't help thinking they could be set to a high tempo metronome."

"Well," Pudding huffed, "that's not necessarily a bad idea now you mention it. A metronome might be a good training tool for spanking girls like you. But there's nothing funny about this punishment you're getting."

Pudding followed that statement up with another round of spanking and Amber couldn't help the words that came spilling out of her mouth a few moments later. "You're not punishing me, though. You just needed to relax, and spanking girls does that for you. I haven't done anything wrong."

"You cheeky little minx!" Pudding cried. "You're just like Candy and Sugar, always denying that you're naughty girls, acting as if you're all sweetness and light. Do you think I don't know you're always getting up to mischief you naughty girl?" Pudding gave her six more spanks. "What do you say to that?"

"I swear, I've done nothing to be punished for. You can spank me if it gets you off, but I've been good, I promise!" Amber protested.

"You little fibber. I don't believe you. I bet you can't get through the morning without doing something naughty. Shall I ask Mistress hmm?" Pudding asked.

Amber shook her head, as her spanking resumed, biting her lip to keep from squealing as Pudding's firm hand punished her bottom.

"I thought not. How gullible do you imagine I am, eh? If Mistress didn't think you needed a punishment, she'd hardly have let me have you, would she?"

Amber wasn't convinced of that, and though she immediately regretted it, she blurted out a denial, "Mistress loves my suffering just as much as you do. That's why she's listening on the phone, so she can hear me getting spanked and enjoy it. She doesn't care if I've done anything wrong, she just needs an excuse to play her games with us."

Pudding gasped in horror. "How dare you! The Mistress would never make up an excuse just to have you, or Candy or Sugar or the ponies punished. Mistress Susanna isn't like that. She's a very fair woman, and she looks after you all, despite your sluttish ways. I don't know what you did, but the fact I'm punishing you for it means you must have done something naughty."

Amber couldn't get out another word as Pudding delivered the next round of spanking. She was too busy howling and squeezing her eyes shut to hold back the tears, with limited success. When Pudding let up the pace to take a few deep breaths, Amber found her body wracked with sobs and her chest heaving as she hauled in great lungfuls of her.

"Yes. You should cry, for saying such unkind things about my Mistress, Amber. You might protest your innocence, my girl, but I know what's really in your heart."

"What's that?" Amber snivelled defiantly.

"You know whatever it was that you did to deserve another punishment from me, though you might deny it. You wanted to be punished for it too, didn't you?"

"No!"

"You offered yourself up as a sacrificial lamb, my dear," Pudding cooed softly.

Amber shook her head. "Don't shake your head, I can tell you wanted to be chastised, it's obvious to me, Amber."

"It's not true," Amber claimed, as tears streamed down her cheeks. Her denial didn't ring true to her, and she didn't think for a minute that Pudding was convinced either.

"Really? Am I mistaken?" Pudding remarked doubtfully. Another smack landed on her cheeks, and Amber blurted, "Yes!"

Pudding's hand didn't leave her cheeks when it landed the next time. Instead, it slipped down the curve of her burning bottom and between her thighs. Amber didn't protest or try to squeeze her legs together. Instead, she parted her thighs to admit the cook's questing fingers which smoothly plunged between her wet lips.

Amber uttered an entirely different type of noise as Pudding's expert fingers parter her sopping wet lips and took charge of her aroused clit.

"In my experience, Amber, a girl who is this wet, is getting exactly what she wanted in her heart, even if she denies it. Would you like to come?" Pudding asked.

"Yes, please, Pudding," Amber admitted, sagging in defeat.

Pudding chuckled, and her fingers performed an intricate dance which had her panting in lust in short order. Amber was soon floating on the edge of a much-needed orgasm, her bottom still fiery from Pudding's disciplinary efforts.

"Admit you deserved this punishment, Amber."

Amber shook her head.

"Admit it, and I'll let you come," Pudding insisted.

Amber shook her head again, but Pudding's fingers held her on the edge of her climax, even when she tried to move her hips to send herself over the edge. The wily cook was playing her like a familiar musical instrument, keeping her in precisely the state she wanted.

"Admit you were naughty, Amber and you can have what you want," Pudding offered.

Amber couldn't take any more of the cook's teasing and gave in, "Yes, I admit it. I deserved my punishment."

"Yes, you did. You're just as naughty as the maids aren't you?"

"Yes, Pudding," Amber groaned, although she wasn't sure that was true. She was pretty sure she had a lot more to learn about being naughty before she could match Candy and Sugar.

"Are you sorry for telling lies about Mistress?"

"Yes, I'm sorry," Amber admitted, this time with the conviction of the truthful. If Mistress Susanna disciplined her or had the staff do so, it was because she needed it. In any case, even if she hadn't bribed Pepper against the spirit of the race, Amber couldn't deny the effect that Pudding's spanking of her bottom had produced.

"Then come for me, you eager little minx," Pudding said, her fingers dancing to a different beat over Amber's aching clit. In a few seconds, she pushed Amber over the cliff into a tremendous orgasm that had her crying out in ecstasy.

Pudding kept her fingers working as Amber rode the wave of repeated orgasms that she demanded from the younger woman. When it was finally done, the cook pushed her off her knee, and Amber found herself on the floor. The older woman reached out with her left hand and took a firm grip of Amber's hair, roughly manhandling her into position. Amber was dragged around, and her head tilted up to look at Pudding, even while she was still coming down from her intense climax.

Without preamble, Amber found her mouth filled with the wet fingers of Pudding's right hand, slick with her own juices and heady with her musk. "Suck my fingers clean. I know you filthy young things love that," Pudding ordered, her eyes flashing with lust as Amber readily complied.

When she was done, Pudding stood up and shrugged quickly out of her dress. Under the simple flowery garment, she wore a set of lingerie that was a stark contrast with the dress that would have looked right at home on the apocryphal 1950's housewife.

Stockings and suspenders were teamed with bra and panties, all matching and all designed to provocatively frame her body and invoke lust in the lucky observer.

"Take off my panties, Amber," Pudding ordered, and the younger woman did as she was told, shuffling forward on her knees and hooking her thumbs into either side of the underwear.

Amber licked her lips as Pudding's pussy was exposed to her gaze and felt a pang of longing as she had to look down and wait for the disciplinarian to step out of the silky panties. Once she had them in her hand, her eyes slid back up Pudding's shapely legs, to the inviting spot the panties had concealed. Amber drank in the sexy view for a brief moment.

It was a struggle to tear her eyes away from Pudding's delightfully bare pussy and the enticing glimmer of arousal that she could see, but Amber just about managed it. On hands and knees, she crossed the room and carefully placed the panties on a large footstool. Naked as she was, that would have given Pudding a great view of her reddened bottom.

That was simply a side benefit of her action, though. The reason she had taken such care was that Pudding's lingerie wasn't a set of garments that should be strewn about the floor, during a rush to get frisky. They were expensive items that needed to be cared for. Even if Amber were inclined to treat a partner's lingerie with casual disinterest, she knew that if the set belonged to her, it would be a treasured item of her wardrobe. Presumably, they were a favourite of Pudding's as she couldn't imagine the cook wearing undergarments like this every day.

Pudding seemed to approve of her care and attention. "Good girl. Now, crawl back over here, and kneel before me."

Slowly, to draw it out, Amber slinked back across the floor, not leaving her hands and knees. She took care to sway her hips and dip her chest low enough that her nipples brushed the carpet.

"Mmm. So you do know how you should behave after all," Pudding said as Amber reached the spot she had indicated and drew herself up on her knees, with her hands behind her, wrists crossed in the small of her back and chest thrust up.

"I'm trying to learn, Pudding," Amber said earnestly, looking down at the cook's expensive, kitten heeled shoes as seemed the most respectful pose to adopt.

"I'm glad to hear it," Pudding replied, stepping forward and slipping a hand into Amber's hair to tilt her head back. She planted her feet either side of Amber's hips and pulled the younger woman's head firmly up between her thighs.

Amber's tongue found Pudding's wet lips, and she was pleased to hear the cook breathe out a sigh of untrammelled lust as she went to work.

"My oh my, you have been learning, haven't you? Is it true that you had never been with a woman until you came into Mistress Susanna's service?" Pudding asked, relenting for a moment on the firm pressure that held Amber's face against her pussy.

Amber took a deep breath and licked her lips, "Yes, Pudding. It's true. I've been missing out on so much."

"Yes, you certainly have been. What a tragedy it is that it took until now for you to experience all that women have to offer you," Pudding lamented. "I'm glad that you now serve our Mistress, Amber. Your tongue is so willing, and you take your punishments well. I'm quite sure that Mistress Susanna is enjoying you a great deal. I do hope you are able to carry out your work duties well. It's frustrating when Mistress has to let a promising girl go because she can eat pussy well but can't manage her actual job."

Amber nodded a fraction in agreement as her tongue continued to lap hungrily at Pudding's delicious pussy. The older woman tasted different from the other staff that Mistress Susanna had ordered her to pleasure. Idly she wondered if there was an equivalent to a wine tasting for pussies. Could an expert tell who she was licking while blindfolded, perhaps?

"Yes, that's really very good for such a short time for you to learn how to eat pussy, my dear. I must commend you on your diligence," Pudding managed to say between moans and deep breaths. Amber's mouth twitched at the corners in a half-smile as she continued to please the cook.

"Oh, yes. Very good indeed. Should you encounter any difficulties in your work, do let me know if I can help, Amber. I worked in a similar field for a while before I found my calling as a cook, and I've worked in enough kitchens and catering jobs to know all about efficiency and productivity. And, of course, self-discipline as well as giving discipline," Pudding chuckled. "Mmmm. I would much rather help you in your free time than allow you to fail to meet the high standards that Mistress sets. Just ask if you think I can help you, I'm positive we can't afford to lose your tongue for want of some skills a personal assistant needs."

Pudding allowed Amber a moment of respite to reply, "Thank you, Pudding. That's a lovely offer, I'll be sure to take you up on it if need be."

"Good. I'm sure that you'll rise to the challenges Mistress sets you and she's an incredibly generous boss. Mistress Susanna takes such good care of us, and the benefits of working for her are amazing," Pudding replied. The older woman had taken Amber's head between her hands now and began to grind her pussy against the submissive's tongue, as she let rip with throaty exhortations to make her come.

Amber was enthusiastic about doing just that. The filthy things that came out of Pudding's mouth as she licked at her seemed entirely at odds with the woman's usual demeanour but turned her on massively. Knowing that Mistress was probably listening to every word added no small frisson of pleasure.

Was Mistress Susanna heading toward her own crescendo, leaned back in her office chair and rubbing at her clit with fingers that were slick with arousal? Would she come at the same time as Pudding, as she heard her cook use her personal assistant's mouth?

The thought of that made Amber wish she could touch herself, but this moment wasn't about her. It was about serving Pudding's needs and through her, serving their Mistress. The spanking had really hurt, and her tormented cheeks rested painfully against her heels as she knelt between the cook's thighs, working her tongue hard and fast against her nub.

It was all worth it, the pain, the embarrassment of being shared like this. Every doubt and moment of anxiety was washed away by the desire to serve her Mistress, and bring pleasure to Pudding so that the party would be a huge success. Amber needed to please Susanna, with every fibre of her being and it was no hardship to do so as the sexual plaything of her boss's cook. Nor, she remembered, would it be a bad thing to serve the ponygirls later. Or the maids if Mistress should choose it.

As Pudding finally began to climax, and her juices ran freely down Amber's chin, she knew that she had found her true calling as Mistress Susanna's lesbian personal assistant.

Amber wondered what else lay in store for her that evening as Pudding pulled her to her feet, and ordered her to pick up her clothes. The clock on the desk showed that they were out of time and the cook shooed her away, bidding her return to their Mistress as she picked up the headset and said, "Thank you, Mistress. That was just what I needed. Amber is on her way to you now."

Pudding flashed a grateful smile at the naked young woman as she hurried from the room.

Amber scurried through the house, naked and anointed with the scent of sex, keen to reach Mistress Susanna's office before her time ran out.

Mistress Susanna must have heard the door to the outer office open because she called out from her own office before they had even shut behind Amber.

"Amber, get in here now, I have need of you," Mistress called out.

Amber knew she was in a state and hesitated for a second before throwing her bundle of clothing on her chair and stepping up to the doors. She would have preferred to clean up, but it wasn't as if Mistress didn't know what she'd been doing just a minute or two ago. If Mistress Susanna wanted her to come in now, making herself look presentable probably wasn't an option.

Amber took a deep breath, straightened up and put her shoulders back, pushing her bosom up, and opened the double doors wide.

"You called, Mistress?" she announced, as she stepped into the office and closed the doors behind her, doing her best to forget the state she was in.

Amber had to turn away from the desk to see her Mistress, who had taken up a position on one of the expensive leather sofas.

Susanna was entirely naked, one foot resting on a plus stool. A stylish and expensive looking phone that would have been at home in the 1920s was on a side table next to her. The handset was off the hook, resting on the table, much as Pudding's had been downstairs, only with a much more expensive phone.

Amber bit her lip as she imagined Pudding listening eagerly on the other end of the line. It was just as delicious a thought as the reverse had been. Was the cook going to hear her punished again, Amber wondered?

"Yes. I want to use your tongue. I do hope Pudding hasn't worn you out. She hasn't, has she?" Mistress Susanna asked, raising a quizzical eyebrow.

Amber shook her head, "No, Mistress. I'm getting quite used to it now."

Susanna nodded, her fingers continuing to work at her pussy. She lifted her other hand and pointed at the floor, swirling her finger around in a circle. "Show me what Pudding has done to you," she ordered.

Amber nodded and came a few steps closer, standing near the foot-stool so that her Mistress could get a good view. She began to turn on the spot, slowly and smoothly, performing a complete revolution and then carrying on until her back was to her Mistress.

To show off her bottom, Amber planted her feet apart, and slowly bent at the waist, leaning forward and pushing her buttocks up as she slid her hands down her thighs until they rested just below her knees.

In this pose, her body was displayed in a particularly lewd fashion, with her pussy and her puckered hole both clearly displayed for her Mistress, who made appreciative sounds. A few moments later, the noise of a digital camera made it clear that Susanna was recording the state of her bottom for posterity.

"Did Pudding hurt your bottom, Amber? You've gone a nice dark shade of pink," Susanna asked.

"Yes, Mistress."

"And you cried, didn't you?"

"Yes, Mistress."

"Did it hurt too much? Was it excruciatingly painful?"

"No, not too much, although it was painful, Mistress," Amber agreed.

"How did you feel about it?"

"I felt. I mean, I was proud, Mistress. To know I was helping Pudding relax and serving you," Amber explained.

"That's good. I want you to be proud of your submission, Amber. If you are suffering for me, I want you to know that it serves a purpose. I don't want you to think I would punish you for no reason," Mistress Susanna said. Amber could hear the faint sound of her Mistress playing with her pussy, the soft, wet noises just audible in the quiet spaces between her remarks.

"I understand, Mistress."

"Good girl."

"Mistress?"

"Yes, Amber? What is it?"

Amber licked her lips and cleared her throat, trying to find the words.

"Spit it out, beautiful. What's on your mind?" Susanna asked forcefully.

"If you wanted to punish me. To hurt me or, make me cry. I mean. If you wanted to spank me or something, but I hadn't done anything wrong. Well. You can do that, Mistress. If it would please you. I'm yours. I want to make you happy, even if I must suffer to do it," Amber stammered.

"Are you asking to be punished for something, Amber?"

Amber shook her head, "No, Mistress."

"Come over here and kneel down young lady," Susanna said. Amber stood up, wobbling a little as the blood rushed to her head. She blinked a few times and shook her head to clear her vision, then turned around and fell to her knees next to the sofa, where her Mistress was pointing.

"What are you telling me, Amber."

Amber swallowed. "That if it gives you pleasure to cane me or flog me, you should, Mistress. You don't have to have an infraction to mind if you want to punish me. I think I," Amber paused and corrected herself, "no, I mean, I know that I like it."

"You like the pain?"

"Not that, Mistress. Not really. I like that you like my pain. I like that you are pleased when I'm obedient. It's exciting," Amber blushed.

"Did you feel the same way about Pudding liking your suffering?" Susanna asked.

"A little, Mistress but mostly it was nice because I knew you wanted it," Amber said. She looked up at Mistress with a sly smile, "And knowing you were listening on the phone was really sexy too."

"I thought you might like that, you naughty little exhibitionist," Susanna laughed. "I'm glad to hear you are so eager to please me, Amber," her Mistress said, sitting up and cupping Amber's chin with fingers wet from her nether lips.

Mistress Susanna leaned forward, and ran her tongue from Amber's jawline, up the trail of salt left by her tears. "Your suffering is delicious, my sweet. Your bottom looks so beautiful. Pudding did a fabulous job on you, and I found listening to you receive such firm discipline wonderfully arousing," Susanna took hold of Amber's hand and guided her assistant's fingers to her wet lips, her eyes never leaving hers. Amber's Mistress kissed her and leaned back, "You can feel how wet I am. That was just from hearing you cry out as Pudding's hand gave your bottom those sweet caresses that you crave so much. How does that make you feel?"

Amber smiled and slipped two fingers deep inside her Mistress, risking not having permission to do so and enjoying the mild surprise on the older woman's face, "I'm happy to be of service, Mistress. If my pain brings you pleasure, I am your willing victim."

Mistress Susanna growled throatily, "I'm so pleased to hear it, you little minx. Do you mean things like this?" Amber gasped as her stiff nipple was pinched and twisted at the same time, giving a little whimper as the pain subsided.

"Yes, Mistress. You're so wet. I hope my pain continues to please you."

"Amber, you are developing so well, I'm proud of your progress. Enough talking. I want my sly tongued slut to please me before dinner," Mistress Susanna said, grabbing Amber's head and roughly pulling her down until her face was buried in her pussy.

"Make me cum, like a good assistant," Susanna ordered.

"Yes, Mistress," Amber said, though the words were muffled by her boss's lips.

CHAPTER 5

"**G**irls, get on the bed and sixty-nine, please. I want you to warm up for Amber and me," Susanna ordered Candy and Sugar. After dinner had been served and a little conversation had passed, Susanna had announced that she had a training session in mind for the evening's amusement.

Amber was still unsure of what it would entail, but they had come up to Mistress Susanna's bedroom, with the maids in tow and she had been ordered to strip them of all their clothing while their Mistress watched.

Susanna and Amber's clothes had followed suit, with Amber disrobing herself and then her Mistress. Her bottom was really quite sore, and Susanna had spent several minutes stroking it and laughing as even light spanks caused Amber to whimper.

Mistress had then taken several more photos of her rosy cheeks, and shown them to Amber on a tablet so she could see how her bottom was still changing colour after Pudding's spanking. She announced her intention to take more photos over the next day or two, so they would have a record of how Amber bruised.

For comparison, Susanna showed Amber some photos of Candy and Sugar, in the same pose, as their bottoms went from their

49

untouched state to coral pink, to maroon and then through the stages of light bruises until they healed up. It was clear that reminiscing over the pictures excited their Mistress, and Amber found herself admiring them as well.

Now all four of them were completely naked with Candy and Sugar enthusiastically entwined in a pussy eating contest. Both of them seemed to be winning, or perhaps losing, Amber thought, depending on one's perspective.

Susanna offered her a harness and helped her step into it. It looked expensive and was surprisingly bulky. The straps were made of leather but padded on the inside, and unlike some she'd seen, the excess length was tidied up with an arrangement of poppers to stop it flapping around. All in all, it was very well thought out.

When Amber had seen strap-on harnesses in videos, they'd often seemed awkward but wearing this one didn't feel that way, even when Susanna showed her the dildos it would be paired with.

"We're going to practice fucking them. Would you like to fuck Candy or Sugar, Amber? This is a treat for you so you can choose."

It didn't really matter to Amber, so she quickly said, "Sugar, please, Mistress."

"Which of these would you like to use?" Susanna said, gesturing at a cupboard she'd opened that concealed a breathtaking array of silicone toys.

Amber looked at them for a while, reaching out to touch a few hesitantly. It was hard to decide. A slim, smooth purple one perhaps? Maybe the significantly larger than seemed plausible one that was otherwise a remarkably realistic imitation of a real cock, down to the colouring of the head and the swollen veins along the shaft.

"I'm really not sure. Which would you recommend, Mistress? For a beginner?" Amber asked.

"This one, if the person you are going to fuck is a beginner themself," Susanna replied, stroking the tip of one of several that were smooth and purple. It was surprisingly small. "It's easy to get carried away and pick a toy that's far too big for a new couple to handle. Particularly if you are going to fuck them in the arse," Susanna said.

Amber swallowed nervously, and Susanna laughed. "Don't worry, there are no hungry bottomed male subs here, thankfully. You'll be thrusting into Sugar's hungry pussy, Amber so it'll be a lot easier. Less warmup and less lubricant. We'll leave fucking arses until you've got a good handle on the rhythm and the technique."

"Oh, good, glad to hear it. So should I pick something medium-sized then, Mistress?" Amber asked, eyeing the extensive collection of silicone.

Susanna nodded. "Yes, about six inches is an ideal length, and it doesn't have to be incredibly thick either, they're a bit firmer than the average real cock, and of course, they never go down. It's better to start with something that is modest and work your way up once you know what you are doing. That leaves the big choice between something smooth like these, the ones that try to be realistic and the exotic shaped ones that have ribs and ridges and lumps and bumps for their pleasure. Oh, and the double-ended models or ones with vibrators of course, but again, we'll leave those for another day. This evening is about learning to fuck a girl and make her come hard, not about how you can get off on it too."

"Would this one be ok?" Amber said, touching her fingertip to a deep purple dildo, that looked about six inches long to her. It was shaped like a real cock complete with a big pair of balls but with some rather wild ridges on the shaft that were based on fantasy rather than human anatomy.

"Yes, not too big or exotic. I wouldn't recommend it if Sugar was new to this, but since she's not, you should be able to fuck her brains out with that. Won't that be nice, Sugar?" Susanna said.

The maid lifted her head from between Candy's thighs and replied, "Yes, Mistress. I can't wait." Sugar winked at Amber and with a lewd abandon, dipped her head back between Candy's thighs.

Susanna watched the wanton display of her maids for a moment before coming back to the present moment and smiling at Amber. "I don't think we'll need lubricant, but we'll use it anyway so you can practice. I'm sure the girls are more than wet enough now. Help me on with my harness, will you dear?"

Amber did as she was told and learned more about how the harness was adjusted. It was easier to see what was going on with another person. Once the harnesses were ready, Susanna selected a large and remarkably realistic looking silicone cock and showed Amber how it fitted into her harness. Then Amber attached her pick to her own harness.

Susanna picked up a paddle and applied it with vigour to Sugar who had the misfortune of being the top girl in the sixty-nine. Or, Amber thought, perhaps the fortune if she liked being paddled. Either way, her cheeks were rosy pink by the time the maids had obeyed their Mistress and licked each other to rather loud orgasms.

Mistress Susanna passed Amber the paddle to put away and ordered the girls onto all fours. Amber got up behind Sugar and looked to her Mistress for instructions.

Susanna had got on the bed in front of Candy and Amber thinking she'd done something wrong made ready to move beside her.

"No dear, you stay behind Sugar and get some lube onto that cock head. I'm going to have Candy demonstrate another way to get a little lube on a strap-on," Susanna said, before offering up the head of her dildo to Candy's welcoming mouth.

The pretty young maid began to fellate the silicone with the lusty abandon both girls employed with all their sexual play. Amber wondered if the girl had ever sucked a real cock, or if she'd learned to be so exuberant purely with Susanna's collection. It certainly looked like she knew what she was doing, as she attacked the dildo with all the tricks that Amber would have tried to use on a guy, just a few short months ago. If she really, really liked him, that is.

"Mistress, why do that?"

"Because I can't feel it, you mean?"

"Yes, Mistress."

"I would say that for many most dominant women, it's about the power and the imagery of it. Candy is sucking a rubber cock, like a good little slut, for her domme. Maybe it's a little about humiliation, maybe it's a demonstration of her submission. It varies from domme to domme. Sometimes it's service to the submissive, giving them something they enjoy for their own needs. If I was using a double-ender I could maybe get a little pleasure from it bu,t I prefer fucking a girl for that," Susanna explained as she let Candy work back and forth on the shaft. "Now, make sure that lube is smeared over the head nicely. That's right. You can line it up with Sugar's pussy now and slowly work it in. I suggest holding the dildo with one hand to guide it, the aiming is more tricky than you think."

Amber did as she was instructed and with slippery fingers, guided the cock into Sugar's welcoming lips. Susanna wasn't wrong about it being tricky. Amber had trouble pushing with her hips and getting the dildo to slide into Sugar, despite how aroused and wet the girl was.

"Try slipping your fingers into her first. Get inside her, then work back and forth a bit, then straighten your fingers up and thrust in and out. You'll be able to work out what angle is right then, it's hard to visualise it for newbies, and if you can't get the cock in her, it's probably because you're pushing the dildo at the wrong angle. Does that make sense?" Susanna asked as she pulled out of Candy's mouth with a plop and moved around the bed.

Amber nodded thoughtfully and found that Sugar was much more easily penetrated with her fingers. Doing as she was advised, she played with the maid for a few moments before getting her fingers straight and then establishing the angle she needed to penetrate the pussy before her with something straight.

"That's good. Can you see what I mean? You need to remember the way the girl you are going to fuck is positioned, of course. Perhaps you've got them bent over the back of a sofa, or on a spanking bench, or they have longer legs than you, and you might need a pillow to kneel on. Maybe you've got their bum up high, but your hand is on their neck, holding the side of their face down in a muddy paddock. Each position they're in affects the position you need to fuck them," Susanna explained congenially.

Her second attempt was much more effective. With a little adjustment of Sugar's hips and switching to kneeling on just one knee, Amber was able to slowly push the dildo into the excited young maid.

Sugar moaned appreciatively as the silicone toy entered her. Amber felt like she had more precise control now.

"That's better, now watch this," Susanna said, taking hold of Candy's hips with both hands and resting the tip of the heavy cock against her lips. Amber wondered how many times she'd have to do this before she could aim one of these things that accurately.

With one slow push, Susanna buried the thick dildo to the hilt in Candy's hungry pussy. The maid let out a passionate groan. "Mmm. That feels wonderful, Mistress," Candy said breathlessly.

Susanna began to draw her hips back and then just before the tip reached her lips, she slowly and smoothly thrust her hips forward again, burying the strap-on in her submissive maid.

"Now, you try. Nice and slow. Pull back until you think you're about halfway out, then slowly back in," Susanna said.

"Yes, Mistress," Amber replied as she began to withdraw the purple silicone from Sugar. She thought she had it just right and was about to change directions, but then the head of the dildo flopped out.

Beside her, Susanna was casually thrusting back and forth, slowly and deliberately. She reached out and patted Amber on the shoulder, "It's ok, sweetie. Get it back in and try again."

Her next attempt was much more satisfying, she managed to build up a bit of a rhythm and slowly fucked Sugar for a dozen or so cycles before she got a bit excited and tried to speed up. That was when the dildo flopped out again, and Susanna laughed.

"Again! Fuck on, fuck off!" her boss said. Sugar and Candy laughed at the reference, and Amber felt her cheeks flushing with embarrassment. Being naked wasn't bothering her, or engaging in lesbian strap-on play with three other women but being made fun off got to her.

Gritting her teeth, she gripped Sugar by the hips and tried to line up the head of the dildo with her pussy. It took longer than she'd hoped, but she finally got it pressed between Sugar's lips. Then she adjusted the maid's knees, bringing her backside down just a bit. That was better.

Amber began to fuck the maid again, and this time, it felt much more comfortable. The dildo slid home with ease, and she didn't pull back far enough for it to pop free. Sugar was soon moaning and groaning with evident delight, and Amber was thrilled with her success.

Grinning wickedly at her, Susanna mouthed, "Watch this."

Reaching forward, Mistress Susanna took a bunch of Candy's hair in her hand and pulled firmly back, lifting the maid's head up as she began to roughly thrust the thick cock back and forth. Candy was mumbling something that was too indistinct to catch, but Amber nevertheless had the distinct impression it was both filthy and approving.

It was hot to watch her Mistress fucking the maid so roughly, and even hotter seeing how much Candy was enjoying having her hair pulled and used as a way to control her and fuck her harder. Amber had to concentrate hard not to go wild fucking her own maid. She was determined not to fumble the cock again.

Amber slapped Sugar's arse, "Why aren't you moaning like that, you little slut?"

"Oh, please, miss. It's nice, really it is," Sugar said.

"I want you to come from it, Sugar, like Candy is," Amber grumbled as Candy grew increasingly excited.

"Yes, miss. I'll do my best," Sugar sighed. Amber frowned as she concentrated and tried to up the pace.

"Fuck me, Mistress, fuck me! Oh. You're fucking me so hard. Sugar, you need it like this. It feels so fucking good. I'm coming!" Candy cried out as she began to climax.

"Lucky cow," Sugar replied, watching her enviously. "Amber needs more practice so she can fuck me good and hard, Mistress."

"Don't be cheeky, Sugar," Susanna said as she pulled out of Candy who contentedly collapsed on the bed, making happy noises.

Susanna moved behind Amber, her strap-on held upright and pressing against her assistant's bottom as she pressed herself up against the younger woman, and wrapped her left arm around her waist. "Let me help you, darling," she whispered in Amber's ear. "Follow my lead."

With that, Susanna took charge of the rhythm of Amber's fucking motion. She pressed her forward with her hips, then guided her back with the hand around her waist. Her right hand brushed up her side and cupped Amber's breast, the fingers playing with her nipple. Mistress Susanna's lips found Amber's neck, and she kissed her softly as she coached one submissive to fuck the other.

Once Susanna had synchronised their movements, she began to speed up the motion. "See baby, you do it like this. Faster," Susanna said before thrusting her hips forward vigorously, causing Sugar to gasp in surprise, "and harder. Just keep it going. Ramp it up slowly. Don't try and pull back too far, short, swift strokes are fine. You'll be able to fuck her with much more length when you get some more practice. For now, let's keep it to short strokes and really get some slapping up against her bottom going, hmm?"

True to her word, Susanna had them thrusting fast and hard until Sugar came a few minutes later. "What do you say, Sugar?" Susanna prompted.

"Thank you, Mistress, and thank you, Amber. That was lovely," Sugar mumbled happily.

"Thank you, Mistress," Amber said as Susanna let go of her, and began to unbuckle her harness.

Her Mistress looked up and frowned, "Come on, get your harness off. We've made them come, now it's their turn to give us pleasure. Girls, on your backs now."

The maids grumbled a bit but rolled onto their backs when Susanna slapped their bottoms and told them to hurry up.

Copying Susanna, Amber moved forward and lowered herself onto Sugar's face, soon feeling the young maid's tongue lapping at her needy clit.

Amber was soon throwing her head back and sighing contentedly as Sugar worshipped her pussy. Susanna reached out and pulled her into a kiss, fondling her breasts as they rode the maids face. That explained why she'd made them lie on the bed head to head, rather than side by side, thought Amber.

"Ride her, Amber. Make her satisfy you. Don't wait for it, take your pleasure from her mouth," Susanna breathed in her ear. Amber looked down to see that her Mistress had one hand twined in Candy's hair and was positively grinding her sex against the maid's flushed face.

"Fuck her mouth with your pussy, Amber. She's a slut just like you are. She'll respond to it," Susanna whispered, smiling triumphantly when Amber obeyed and began copying her motions.

Sugar moaned into her pussy as she worked her tongue over Amber's sex.

Susanna glanced down at Sugar's face, "See, what did I tell you? Sugar loves to be ridden like this, don't you sweetie?"

Sugar said something that sounded agreeable but was muffled by the wet lips pressed hard against her mouth.

"Candy too. I've trained them both to enjoy the finer things in life," Susanna said. "Just as I'm going to train you."

"Yes, Mistress. She's really going to town," Amber said.

"Feels good, doesn't it? To take control of them and take what you want?"

"It does, yes. Sugar is so gifted with her tongue, Mistress," Amber replied, stumbling over her words as she began to come hard, shuddering and shaking over the maids face. Her thighs trembled as her orgasm ripped through her. "Sugar, that was glorious," she sighed.

Susanna reached for her again and kissed her deeply as she rode Candy's face to her own orgasm.

They collapsed on the bed, leaving the maids licking their lips and dozing contentedly.

"Did you enjoy your orgasm?" Susanna asked.

"Yes, Mistress, it was perfect."

"Don't forget you're spending tomorrow evening serving at the pleasure of my ponies though," Susanna pointed out.

"I hadn't forgotten, Mistress. I'm looking forward to it," Amber replied happily.

"Are you indeed?" Susanna said, with obvious amusement.

"Yes, Mistress."

"Interesting. You do understand that Pepper and Ginger are probably going to torment you and they're unlikely to let you come, don't you?" Susanna said with a laugh.

"Yes, Mistress but that's alright," Amber said.

"How so?"

"Well, I won the race, so I'm due to collect my prize of an orgasm anyway, right?"

Susanna sat up with a start. "Are you perfectly serious, young lady?" she snapped.

Amber sat up and shrugged, "I thought that was the deal."

"But you cheated!" Susanna protested.

"Cheating is a bit of a strong word. I just offered some encouragement and Pepper raced her little socks off," Amber pointed out.

"So you think you're due a prize?"

"Yes I do," Amber said confidently.

That was when Susanna pounced. She flipped Amber onto her back, making her shriek in surprise.

With a growl, Susanna claimed her mouth, kissing her passionately. Then she began working her way down Amber's body, kissing her neck, the swell of her breasts and then nibbling and sucking hungrily at her pert nipples.

The trail of kisses passed down her chest and over her stomach, and then Susanna slipped her arms under Amber's knees and hauled her legs up, pushing them back toward her shoulder. Her Mistress rolled her up, so her knees ended up on either side of her head, then placed her mouth on Amber's pussy, her tongue dipping between her wet lips and her mouth hungrily sucking on her clit.

Amber purred in delight.

"I'll give you your prize, you cheeky little slut. I'm going to give you the best orgasm of your life," Susanna boasted. Amber bit her lip and moaned as her Mistress put her tongue to work. She writhed under the agile tongue of her Mistress for quite a few moments before she was able to get enough of a grip on herself to lift her head and reply.

"Yes, Mistress."

AUTHOR'S NOTE

Thank you for reading Raced by Her Lesbian Boss, Book Four of the Submissive Lesbian Personal Assistant series.

If you enjoyed the book and can spare the time to leave a review on Amazon or Goodreads, I would greatly appreciate it.

Positive and constructive feedback and comments, even a simple star rating, are a great way to let me know that you want to read more about these characters.

This series is about Amber, and the other women in service to Susanna Hamilton, a wealthy lesbian with a hedonistic lifestyle.

Miss Hamilton has a taste for games of domination and submission, and employs Amber to be her new Personal Assistant.

Amber has never gone beyond an active fantasy life, and actually played with another woman. Susanna offers the twin temptations of a much needed job and pleasures Amber has never tasted.

I have plans for a quite a few books in this series as we join Amber on her journey of sexual experimentation. Don't forget to let me know if you want me to prioritise writing more of the Lesbian Boss series.

Thanks for your support, and for buying the book or borrowing it through Kindle Unlimited.

AUTHOR'S NOTE

Yours steamily,
K.F. Jones

ALSO BY K.F. JONES

The Consort of the Werewolf King is the first series by K.F. Jones and follows a young English biology student, who is bitten by a wild wolf.

His friends and colleagues insist that there are no wolves in the UK. William's hunt to prove he was not imagining things leads him to meet, Brian, a local landowner who may be more than he seems.

Consort of the Werewolf King

Bitten by the Alpha - Book 1

Claimed by the Alpha - Book 2

Trained by the Alpha - Book 3

Initiated by the Pack - Book 4

Other work by K.F. Jones

Dawn and the Galvanic Capacitor

Dawn and The Pilferer's Punishment

Dawn and the London Society

Dawn is a bounty hunter, bodyguard and private detective in a steampunk world full of adventure, excitement and lusty antics.

The Tribulations of Dawn will follow our heroine as she tries to reclaim a stolen item for her employer. The Professor is at the forefront of research into advanced steam technology, and his invention could change the world for good or ill.

Dawn has a wandering, and somewhat lascivious eye, to match her quick wit and mean right hook. Woe betide the thieves when she catches them.

But can she be well-behaved for long enough to safely return the gizmo to the Professor? Or will it slip through her fingers and send her off on the chase again?

Submissive Lesbian Personal Assistant

This is a new series about Amber, a young woman who is seduced by her new employer, a dominant and wealthy lesbian.

Punished by Her Lesbian Boss

Seduced by Her Lesbian Boss

Trained by Her Lesbian Boss

ABOUT THE AUTHOR

K.F. Jones is writing in two main worlds. The first is about a young man who finds love in the arms of an older werewolf with a kinky streak. The Consort of the Werewolf King features some very naughty werewolves, that no amount of discipline will tame.

The second is all about strong, confident young women capable of taking on any challenge, in a sexy steampunk world. You'll meet Dawn first, and follow her as she tries to make up for a mistake made while she indulged her passions.

Later you'll meet Mercy, who should be studying at the Academy and concentrating on her exams. If she could just avoid regular disciplinary sessions in the Deputy Head's office, or find a way to keep the demanding Headmistress satiated, perhaps she could finally unravel the conspiracy she's discovered!

If you'd like to find out when new books are released, join the mailing list at the website. **http://kfjones.net/**

twitter.com/kfjonesauthor
facebook.com/KFJonesbooks
pinterest.com/kfjonesauthor
goodreads.com/kfjones
amazon.com/author/kfjonesbooks